FROM ROAD
TO
DESTINATION

JIYA VORA

ISBN 9789354389818
© JIYA VORA 2021
Published in India 2021 by Pencil

A brand of
One Point Six Technologies Pvt. Ltd.
123, Building J2, Shram Seva Premises,
Wadala Truck Terminal, Wadala (E)
Mumbai 400037, Maharashtra, INDIA
E connect@thepencilapp.com
W www.thepencilapp.com

DISCLAIMER: *The opinions expressed in this book are those of the authors and do not purport to reflect the views of the Publisher.*

Author biography

"Success Or Failure?"
What you will name it-
because first failure and first achievement both says one thing:

" IT IS JUST A BEGINNING "

I am a sixteen year old girl,from surat,gujarat.
from last two years, I am writing poems and quotes which make me understand the mystries of life-
What is success,
What is Failure,
What is hope,
What is courage,
What is love,
and What is LIFE!
my all questions, answer I have revealed in this book.
This is my second poetry book.
And at last, I am very thankful to my parents-VAIBHAV VORA and HETAL VORA to support me,to inspire me and to understand my dreams.

MAIL: jiyavora47@gmail.com
Instagram : _from.bottom.of.heart_
facebook: Jiya Vora

CONTENTS

A DAY OF LIFE!

ONCE I WAKE UP IN THE MORNING AND THOUGHT-
A DAY OF MY LIFE BRINGS ME A LOT!
WITH MY PASSION, I BEGIN IT WITH AN INTENTION,
AND THAT TAKES ME ONE STEP CLOSER TO MY DESTINATION.
AND FINALLY DAY BRINGS A LOT TO ME,
SOMETHING TO LEARN,
SOMETHING TO REMEMBER,
SOMETHING TO FOUND,
SOMETHING TO ACCEPT.
I NEVER WANT TO WAIT FOR A RIGHT TIME TO ARRIVE,
BECAUSE CHANCE IS NOT WHAT YOU GET ,
IT IS SOMETHING YOU CREAT!

AN INVISIBLE HAND

1.
A long time passed,
Since I heard your voice,
We never met again after that gloomy night.
Along with your memories, what I know forever is,
You will be always here holding my arms like an invisible
hands!

STRENGTH I HAVE

2.
Sitting under the stars,
I often thought about that fearful past.
Even today, whether I win or lose,
Always keep inspiring myself about the strength I have.

WORTH!

3.
Hiding your tears, don't show other that fake smile.
Behind unexposed truth, never let them to play with your
feelings which they never worth.
Don't change yourself for their want of while,
Trust me , being like yourself you are always worthwhile!

IT'S RARE

4.

When you throW away all the obstacles which is between in your way,

And again move on for the dreams which you once decided to achieve them.

MILES AWAY!

5

On that evening, it was our last talk.
With the painful end, everything remain untold on it's way.
Even today, feeling your presence in every maze,
But the fact is, we are miles away.

WHAT WILL THEY SAY!

6

Never bother about what the world will say,
Never hurt about those people's question.
Just continue your work,
Because it is your success which answer them one day.

DREAM!

7

I remember that night when I decide my goal.
And on the next morning, I don't know from where this strength comes to me.
I don't know where this aspiration takes me,
But what I know for sure is,
I will get a reason to live my life.

DESIRE TO FLY!

8
How if I could born with wings?
How if I could fly joyfully in open sky.
Out of all those worries,
Thinking between ifs and why,
But I never let give up my desire to fly.

HOPE!

9
It's rare!
Feeling very numbness and desolate,
I departure a journey to find a hope.
Seeking it in every maze,
But I finally find it inside myself.

BELIEVING

10.
Trusting you is like,
Closing the eyes in the day and feeling presence of night.
We got lost in the mirage.
Trusting you,
Once out of all the mirages,
We will together soon.

AGAIN!

11
Not you,
 I just want your solace for my exhausted mind and to
settle down chaos.
And your smile to unlock my happiness and to make me
smile once again!

SATISFACTION

12.
Being happy with something,
Never complain about having little.
Instead of bother I don't have,
Just enjoying something I achieve.

YOUR DREAM!

13

A day doesn't mean just for rest and joy,
But for scuffle and sacrifice for achievement of your
dream!

FROM BEGINNING!

14.
That hard work,
That struggle,
That sacrifice,
And a hope in your dreams.
Once you will surely achieve success,
Which you worth from beginning!

FRIEND LIKE YOU!

15.
Many heys,
Many handshakes,
And finally many goodbyes.
A number of people I met on my way.
But I never have the friend like you,
Because it is very fortunate to get.

UNITY UTMOST!

16.
This mind has seen many disputes and wars,
But this heart of mine still believes in the glory of unity
utmost!

MIRROR MAZE!

17.
Miles I have passed,
In seeking the success.
Without losing hope, further I stepped,
In every mirror maze.

ANYTHING TO AFRAID

18.
Nothing more to reveal,
Nothing more to scared,
Thinking about the past,
Is there anything to afraid?

WHAT YOU CHOOSE!

19.
Like a wind ,
Once time whispered in my ears and said me,
"I will give you both-
The bad memories of past and the peace of present.
It is upon you, what you choose!"

ACHIEVEMENT!

20.
What strength without fear,
And what ardency without endeavor.
What sunshine without darkness,
And what dream without achievement?

ILLUSION!

21.
Stick seems like sword ,
And stone seems like mountain.
Fear overwhelmed my body,
Is there any solution , that I can remove my illusion.

DONT' KNOW WHERE

22.
Black clouds all around,
Don't know when sun will shine.
Sadness is all around,
Don't know where happiness I hide?

CLOSE TO YOU!

23.
We are miles apart from each other,
But when I started writing about you,
Those words took me close to you!

I WANT TO ACHIEVE

24.
It took day and night of mine,
Did hardwork and built some strength , I believe
But now, just seeking for a chance.
Because there is something I want to achieve!

FREEDOM UTMOST!

25.
This mind has bears pain and heard groans,
But this heart of mine still believes in glory of freedom
utmost!

MILES APART!

26.
I often thought about that rainy day.
Under the tree, The ring you gave,
And after that how childish I behave.
Your last gift feels like your presence,
Feels like we are too closer.
but unfortunately , we are miles apart!

FORGET YOU!

27.

It brought tears in my eyes when I remember our last talk.
Even I know, you still not forget those last words I spoke.
The fact is just for a short while we were together.
But trust me,
 Instead of Remembering , It become so hard for me to forget you.

INSIDE MYSELF !

28.
Felling very numbness and desolate,
I departure a journey to find hope.
seeking it in every maze,
But I finally find it inside myself!

WHICH WAS NEVER MADE!

29.
Alone on the bridge,
With an hope,I am passing through it.
With an imagination, that bridge will fill distance between
those two mountains.
And I endeavour to achieve the success.
But on the bridge,
Which was never made!

TO SACRIFICE

30.
Being delicate, She is sharp like sword.
With plenty of courage,
And abudant of strength.
forgetting herself, for her loved ones,
And working for them day and night. but she will never let
her dream to sacrifice!

THAT FAILURE!

31.

Seeking an Opportunity door,

I wish that I find it soon.

And when I get the door, I will open it by my key of hard work.

And I will fulfill all those desire which was born by that failure!

I HAVE TO FACED!

32.
Still there is something more to achieve,
Still there is something more to adage,
One thing what I need is courage,
To accept all those conflicts which I have to faced!

TIME I END!

33.
Tired of the day ,
While sitting under the stars,
I throwback in that time when I start.
I remind myself about
 my sacrifice,
 my struggle ,
and my need,
And that what I did for my dream.
In those days, I never forget
 what I have to achieve,
what I need to fulfill,
 And finally I find that one day.
 and now I come back in the time I end!

ME AND MYSELF

34.
Every breath of mine I am just remembering the time I
spend with you.
 There is no words to describe our relation.
 From you, companion and love I learned and all the
memories of my fearful past I burned.
Many form of your,
 sometimes my courage,
 my strength,
and sometimes my support and solace.
 I remember the promise I gave.
And even the remarkable talks we have
 You will be always there inside me like a soul.
 That is how bond between Me and myself.

I ALWAYS SCATTERED

35.
Success or failure or that what I always scattered.
 Nights have been passed in thinking about my fruitful results.
Fear of nothing yet everything.

Every morning,I wake-up with a new   inspiration which takes me once they closer to my destination.
 all those struggles,
All those hard work,
 Always bring something for me to learn .
Apart from taking me near success,
There is something to forget and something to accept .
Success or failure,
Or that what I always scattered!

PROMISE!

36.

Remembering you,

Every moment, I like to just remembering you and our memories.

That is true,

we are no longer together to make new memories,

And to laugh joyfully with each other.

Even today your non-appearance fill my heart with desolate,

Tears makes their way through my eyes,

Every moment yelling your name deep inside.

Remembering you,

You will be always there in my heart,

because we made promise to love each other until we die!

IN THE OPEN SKY!

37.

Time passed away,

Sometime it passes in those childhood pranks,

So sometime in scattering and happiness.

Sometimes in fighting with friends,

So sometime in struggling for success.

In the morning, I usually missing that casual kiss of my father.

It became a blessing which makes my day.

And sometimes i'm seeking that miracle in food which lies in my mother's hand.

Time passed away,

 just has wind blowed in the open sky!

WHO WILL UNDERSTAND MY PROBLEM!

38.
Cannot bear this any more,
I abandon to reveal Myself.
I gave up to talk about conflict I faced.

Many people asked me why I am not adaging like earlier?
 They want to know secrets behind my silence.

 But in this world is there any trustful person to
understand my problem?

PAST!

39.

Nights I have passed in thinking- how wonderful If I
 could stop complaining about past and live joyfully in
present.

My past gave me to remarkable things-
A moment which has abudent of happiness.
Or A moment which left those unhealed scars .
 It's upon me what I choose!
And how wonderful If I could heal those left marks and I
enjoy present without scared about my past!

WHERE I WANT TO!

40.
Somewhere!
Every morning,
 when day breaks continue I begin with what I end last night.
 I don't know from where it comes to me.
I don't know where it will take to me.
I don't know what it will bring to me.
But what I know for sure is,
 it will take me somewhere , where I want to!

YOU FOREVER!

41.

I want your hand for solace and support.
 Your hand ,
 to clean my all the years which is rolling down my eyes.
Your hand,
to hold my hand and make me realise that you will be always there for me .
And your hand ,
to begin a journey around the world with you forever!

ANSWER THEM ONCE!

42.
frustrated of it,
I cannot bear this taunts any more .
At night when I entered in my room,
 darkness surrounded me.
 Feeling very numbness and desolate I fallen down.
Nobody knows but I just need a solace to stand once
again.
 On the next day,
 Ignoring all the taunts and teasing of yesterdays,
I begin with my heart work .
That is how ,me and my success will answer them once!

COMES TRUE!

43.
It's rare!
When apart from that desolate,
 you again sow seeds of inspiration in your heart.

 It's rare!
 forgetting your Failure,
 you again step further to achieve the Success.

 It's rare!
In the darkest night,
 You doesn't lose hope for ray of light.

 And it's rare!
when all these doesn't more remain as an imagination and
comes true!

LOVE! LOVE! LOVE!

44.

Love. Love. Love!
Sitting under the sky,
 looking towards cloud and suddenly I fallen in love with
nature.

Love. Love. Love!
In the morning, when day start and I get a new inspiration
and I fallen in love with myself.

Love. Love. Love!
Achieved something.
And suddenly all the chaos of my mind settle down.
And feeling abudent of happiness.
 And that is how I fallen in love with my life.

 Love. Love. Love Everywhere!

I MAKE IT FULFILL!

45.
Little makes everything,
 Happy with something I am not rushing towards all the
luxuries.

 Desire of doing something yet everything.
Enjoying and satisfied with whatever I have.
Not crying for anything if I am not able to achieve.
 little makes everything,
Hope soon,I make it fulfill!

PROMISE ME!

46.

I will bear your pain with the strength I have.
 promise me,
 you will accept me ,
Facing all the challenges you have!

I will always be there for you, holding your hand with
affection I have.
promise me,
you will love me with the care you have!

LOST YOU FOREVER!

47.
From when you have gone,
 I know you will come soon,
but somewhere I am very miserable,
 that I have lost you forever.

That handshake when we met first,
Seems like we will always there for each other.
 But that bye ,
make me fear that I have lost your forever.

what should I do?
 just praying to god to protect you every foe.
 Without you spending every moment with your solace and
hope!

NOT COME YET!

48.

Everyday ,

doing the same hard work but don't know when it will finish.

I just continue to move on but don't know when I will reach to my success with same spirit.

 being started I am praying for its successful end,

 that is how I am thinking about the time which has not come yet!

DISAPPEARED

49.
Is there anything more to asked,
 Is the anything more to reveal,
I just showed them out ,
which once lies in my courage!

 Proof of my sacrifice,
and secrets of my struggles,
I just want to show them my strength ,
which ones get hide but never get disappeared!

MEMORIES!

50.
Memories seems like a frame made up of happy moments
and hang on the wall .

Memories seems like those tiny and silly mistake you did
among all.

Memories seems like those cheerful moments of earlier
make you smile casually in present.

 And forgetting all bad incidents of past,
memories makes sense to all apart!

PASSED AWAY!

51.

Passed away that was the time when we were together in every circumstances.

Passed away that was the time when we used to have those sad- happy talks at the night .

Passed away that was the time,
 When you never forget that casual smile of mine the morning.

 Passed away that was the time, when you leaved my hand, which you once hold to promise
That we are together forever!

DESTINATION!

52.
People able to see or not,
 but your struggle reflect in your work.
They able to listen or not,
 but your success shouted all over the world.

 Passing with time ,I have some aspiration .
At every step I give my talent's examination.
 because of it, I have some isolation,
but it last, Finally I reached to my destination!

REST OF YOUR LIFE!

53.
If you fallen for once,
You will not Hurt for it .
But If you lost the strength to stand once again,
 then you will sorry for rest of your life!

NOT MY LOVE!

54.

Those rainy days of our togetherness,

I am missing in my loneliness. Time pass away on its way,

 and we got our opposite maze.

 Not you but even fortunate with memories of yours I have,

Always remember that you have just lost me not my love!

ALONG WITH THE MAZE!

55.
It will take day and night of yours,
 it will take strength and struggle of yours ,
but once if it will come ,
It will definitely give you the fame you deserve!

 Starting from today,
 begin to find its way,
Many obstacles you will get,
 but it will solve down along with the maze!

AROUND THE WORLD!

56.
Thinking about you which I am doing nowadays .
Missing you and feeling loneliness I always.
I don't know how to hide this, because gone was the time
when I used to open and expose around the world!

NEVER GIVE UP!

57.

Don't be sorry for yourself ,

be sorry for the people who are thinking you can't do that

again.

 Very confident,

 Very proudly,

Just show them what is there lies in your Power behind!

IS THERE ANYONE!

58.
Is there anyone?

 Feeling very regret and sorrowful for the mistakes I did ,
but I want to ask,

 Can you give me a chance
 to explain why I did so.
 Is there anyone to listen and understand the reason
behind?
 Is there anyone who want to know whole truth instead of
the half?
Even today she's facing many conflicts,
but is there anyone to make her safe to explain herself?

TO ACHIEVE THE SUCCESS!

59.
Bother with daily routine,
 Tired with my daily struggling,
 but when I remember my dream and aim,
 I think, This all is just about few days and I have to work
hard to achieve the success.

NEAR TO MY SUCCESS!

60.
Nights are witness of my hard work and struggles ,
That new sunrise knows all the secrets of my old ambition.
Everyday I have many challenges to accept,
but by solving it,
I feel I am going near to my success.

TIRED OF EVERYTHING!

62.

Tired of everything,

Each and every thing which I am just doing for them.

Crying but nobody knows except my eyes.

Laughing but hiding my all the tears inside.

Pain haven't healed out But I just Hide them all about!

Tired of everything,

Just need a solace to make me relax once again.

A JOURNEY!

63.
Starting a journey ,
with my courage, I am moving towards my destination.
Meeting Many people at every station and have some memories.
 but as way divides, we leave each other for our dream and aspiration.
With my strength,
 On my way , I'm facing all the obstacles.
HOPE, soon I will reach to my destination!

PROVE YOURSELF!

64.
Heal your all the pains
Forget the consequences of defeat,
 Because tomorrow is the new chance to prove yourself.

UNTIL WE MEET AGIN!

65.
I remember,
How we became happy, laughing together at those small matters.
How your Presence makes my day and slowly it became a reason behind my happiness.
Even Today,
When your absence,
Your non- appearance fill my heart with desperate,
But It is your memory that makes me smile once again.
The fact is, we're no longer together will certainly cause me pain.
Amidst the crowd, I desolate.
Tears rolling down my cheeks.
Every moment,
Just yelling your name deep inside,
With the Hope that you would once come back.
And never forget, you'll be always there in my heart,Until we meet again.

IT'S MIRACLE!

66.

It's miracle!

When you learn to spend time alone, Far away from that throngs where you certainly feel incomplete and lone.

Be fond of every moment of life,

And keep reminding yourself that everything will fall to it's place some day.

And, When Sitting under the stars,

Apart from omission, you always try to sow seeds of motivation in your heart.

It's become a miracle, when you make sense to all!

SOLITUDE!

67.
It 's magic !
When you learn to live alone,
Spending time with your own self,
 and enjoy your own company.
Away from that crowd where you generally
feel incomplete and solitude!

UNTIL WE DIE!

68.

On that despair night, Everything Faded away.

Under the hill, The words you spoke,

Hurt me the most.

I know, There was a untold reason behind turbulent words.

There was some circumstances behind we left each other.

You are the most trustful person from my sight,

Because we made a promise to love each other until we die.

HOME!

69.
Travelling along,
Or that what I always think of.
Many peoples meet at every station of life and have some
memories,
But is there anything home like?
A home,
To catch the sight of world from that window.
A home,
To turn your experience into an Unforgettable story.
A home,
to laugh Stupidly and to reveal your childish nature.
Travelling along,
I often thought that is nothing home like!

THE WORDS YOU SPOKE!

70.
Turning around,
Or that what I always scared of!
Cannot deny the lie and even don't have a strength to
accept it.
Behind hiding the truth, your silence hurt me every
moment.
Whether truth or lie ,
right or wrong,
I just believe the words you spoke! Turning around,
I made a promise to trust you from heart's core,
And I will just believe the words you spoke.

NEVER FEAR TO DREAM

71.
Never fear to Dream!

Because if you are capable to dream
something,
Then you're surely worthy to achieve it.

REVEAL MYSELF!

72.
Writing down emotions on an empty page,
That's how I feel I have reveal myself.
Poured my thoughts and portrait every Ups-downs I Faced.
And slowly I opened every secrets in those poems I penned.

I ASKED FOR!

73.
Flying in the sky,
That's how accepting all the challenges which world offers
every next day.
Out of all those worries,
In my thrill,
My heart touch little moment of happiness every now and
then.
All the Chaos get settle down and mind is at peace,
Always fulfilling every Desire,
Instead of confused between Ifs.
Flying with wings,
It seems Joy is in the air,
Flying in the sky,
Or that what I always asked for.

YOUR...!

74.
Not worldy objects,
Not even luxurious life.
What I always want is,
Your hand to hold and fulfilling every desire together.
Your shoulder to lean on in scary moments.
And your heart to trust me each and every day.
That what I always asked for!

MOVING THROUGH THE FACT!

75.
Moving through the fact,
Or That what I always afraid.
All the worries,
 All the Chaos,
I think I have lost the strength to faced them all.
Cannot even accept the fact and do not deny the lie.
Feeling very numbness,
Everything got turbulent on its way,
Don't know where the strength gone.
 but I need a solace to stand again.
Moving through the fact,
Or that what I always afraid.

WITHOUT FEAR!

76.
Not all the time,
People want advice for their mistake.
What they eagerly want is,
Your presence to listen their silence.
 Your hand to dry all tears.
Your heart to understand them.
And a shoulder to lean on without fear.

WRITE AGAIN!

77.
Many things are still remain to reveal.
Still remain to sketch words on empty page.
Still remain to portrait glories with pen.
 And still remain to open the secrets in the poem I penned.
I wish I could write again.

I PENNED!

78.
Sitting under the stars,
I often poured my heart on an empty page.
I often let my thoughts to flow with pen.
I often reveal all the secrets hiding in the maze,
And I often portrait our memories in the poems I penned!

UNDER THE STARS!

79.
A moment happens,
When you calm down all the chaos of the mind,
and let your heart to touch a little moment of happpiness
by its side.
when you stop rushing yourself in the memories of past,
and never give-up your desire and dream.
Often thinking while sitting under the stars!

FACE THEM ALONE!

80.
Never hurt about those people questions.
Not even bother what the world will say.
just forget them all!
because it is only you and your work which face them
alone!

GROWING UP!

81.
Growing up,
That how, missing those days we have spent,
And thinking about the time which has not come yet.
Busy with all our dreams and aspirations ,
And that how we got our different destinations.
remembering those memories,
that how I feel I have lost my wonderful days.
And growing up,
For the time which has not come yet.

I DID FOR IT!

82.
Nights have been passed,
Thinking; How if I could born with Wings.
One cannot stop me from flying in the colourful sky,
And screaming joy loudly.
But in the morning,
I fly with my dreams Because of Courage and work I did
for it.

WHERE SHOULD I GO AHEAD!

83.
Where should I go ahead?
On my way towards success,
I got confused when road divide.
Many questions, My achievement which road has?
 Don't know where should I go ahead!

 After sometime I got scattered,
 disturbed between two roads ,
I decided I never let my desire to give up.

 Life give me multiple choices
Its upon me what I choose.
Confused between two maze,
Hope, Soon I will reach to my success.

I GREW UP!

84.
Childhood
I grew up!
Surrounded by all those fairy tales and nightmares.
It's wonderful!
At very small age, an abundant of world's happiness I knew.
And with strategy to climb the step of the success I grew.

With no destination but have some aspirations.
 Even today my childhood strength give me some inspiration.

Nothing more I need,
 Just that stressless smile of my childhood.
And those memories of my friend with whom I grew!
 I grew up!

FOREVER!

85.
Not in the sky,
 Not only on the land,
I will always there with you,
In every mirror maze.

Holding you tightly in my arms,
 I want to travel throughout the world.
 Whether the time is difficult or unmiserable,
I will not leave your hand forever!

SHE HAVE TO FACED!

86.
Accepting all the challenges which
 world offers her every Next day.
Fulfilling her all the Dreams for what
 she is always struggling.
Many forms of her,
Always fulfilling every Desire of her
 loved one without any question.
Not even she came first for herself,
Give priority and even care more for
 her loved one.
She is brave,
Always fight alone
against the conflicts she have to faced.

WITH THE TIME!

87.
It took a moment of mine,
To forget all those chaos of mind and let my heart to be
filled with happiness in deep ocean of miles.

 This moment is only moment,
 it will never return back.
This sadness and pain lies ,
it will be also disappeared along with the time!

GOAL!

88.

Goal needs a precise stagnation in mind.

Whether in time of growing up quality or in time of passing through hurdles in between maze!

EVERY PROSPECT

89.
An unexposed time!

how slowly it had been passed,
to Heal our all the pains and to make us stand to bounce
back.
And sometimes, how fast it goes,
to let us touch every small moment of happiness .
Whether It was a failure or an achievement,
It was a bad incident on a good willing,
 Along with the time we just remember or forget it.
I never exposed anything about it,
Not even let anyone to know what is it!
 Always hiding inside like a secret,
but it was the time which changed me in every prospect.

JOURNEY!

90.
On the Journey?
The courage which you are seeking outside lies right inside you.